Nick the Wise Old Cat is offered as a series of life-lesson stories and value messages as seen through the eyes of a "wise old cat" and a nice lady guardian. It is the author's hope that each series will serve as an educational seed that will establish or reinforce cherished values within our children and influence positive developments in their moral and social character.

- Nick the Cat, LLC

Library of Congress Cataloging-in-Publication Data
Sicks, Linda M.

Nick the Wise Old Cat Series created and written by Linda M. Sicks.
All illustrations created by Dave Messing/All illustration rights owned by Nick the Cat, LLC.

How I Found My Family
ISBN 978-1-936193-00-4
Library of Congress Control Number: 2009935187

Book Design, Marketing and Project Director
Keith D. Ramundo

Printed in China by BookMasters, Inc.
Kowloon, Hong Kong
Printed October 2009
Reference Number A10

All rights reserved. Published by Nick the Cat, LLC.
Printed and Distributed by BookMasters, Inc.
30 Amberwood Parkway, P.O. Box 388, Ashland, Ohio 44805
800-537-6727   419-281-5100   Fax: 419-281-0200
info@bookmasters.com   www.bookmasters.com

Author's Dedication:

Without Nick and Baby Z in my life, I would not have this story to tell.

Without the warm and creative illustrations by Dave Messing, the heartfelt expressions of this story would not have been captured.

Without Keith Ramundo's creative direction, his continuing inspiration, and unlimited patience and humor, we all would have missed out on this wonderful experience.

I am truly grateful for having all of you in my life!

L.S.

Hello, my name is Nick and I am a BIG, VELVETY,
BLUE - GRAY CAT. I have been told I am a wise old cat, for I have seen
and done many things. Let me share with you how I found my family.

HOW I FOUND MY FAMILY

Book One of Three in Series 1
"The Importance of Family" from the
"Nick the Wise Old Cat" Book Series

When I was just six weeks old, my mother's family, the Ramseys, decided to move. They were an older couple who wanted to sell their big house and move into a small condo. The condo allowed only one cat to live there. Mother understood the situation. She explained to my sister and me that families don't always stay together.

She said, "When I was a kitten, I found my new family at a pet store. But that was many years ago, and finding a family today is very different than it was back then."

She told us that her family's friend, Frank, helped homeless animals find special homes. Frank had a business where people came to find small animals like birds, fish, hamsters, and EVEN SNAKES, to join their families.

While Frank loved all of the animals in his shop and enjoyed helping each family find a special pet, he worked especially hard to find homes for abandoned cats and dogs in need of rescue.

Frank knew there were many cats and dogs that had trouble finding a family to love. Some of these animals were strays that didn't belong to anyone. Some were puppies and kittens born to dogs and cats that were homeless. Others were older dogs and cats that had lost their families along the way.

Feeling that every animal was special, Frank made room for these homeless dogs and cats. They could stay with Frank until they were adopted by families who wanted a pet to love. Mother told us we would stay at Frank's shop until we found our new home.

At Frank's, my sister and I were placed in the same space. That was nice because we could be together and talk about what kind of family we wanted to live with and love.
We talked also about how we might not get to live with the same family.

That was okay; we remembered our mother telling us that families don't always live together. She said we were meant to belong to new families where we could grow and learn new ways, but most important, share our love with others. This was all exciting to me, for I knew I had a lot of love in my heart to give my future family.

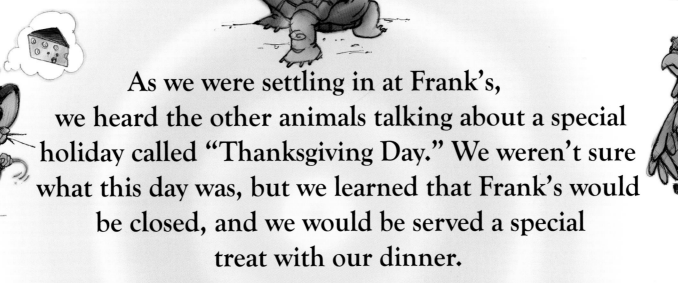

As we were settling in at Frank's,
we heard the other animals talking about a special
holiday called "Thanksgiving Day." We weren't sure
what this day was, but we learned that Frank's would
be closed, and we would be served a special
treat with our dinner.

Many of the animals talked about how excited they were for
Thanksgiving. They couldn't wait to see what special
treat they might receive. The bird was dreaming
about juicy grapes. The puppies
hoped for bones. All the animals
had some special treat in mind
and could hardly wait for the
holiday to arrive.

Later that morning, a woman and a little girl walked into Frank's and stopped right in front of us. They kept talking to my sister and me. The little girl liked my sister's white, fluffy fur and said that she looked like a snowball!

The puppy next to us said, "I think your sister has found her family."

I asked, "What do you mean?"

He said, "I saw this earlier in the morning with my brother and his new family. You see, these families come into look at us, hold us, get excited, and start talking about what they want to name us. I am sure she is getting a family," he repeated.

Sure enough, that is exactly what was happening. While her new family was buying food and toys to take home, my sister and I looked at each other, hugged, and licked each other good-bye. We said that although we would miss each other, we were happy to have a chance to learn, grow, and offer love to others. She assured me it would be just a matter of time before my new family would come into Frank's and adopt me.

When I woke up the next morning, all the other animals were again talking about Thanksgiving and the special treat they would be receiving tomorrow with their dinner.

Just before noon, one of the birds left with his new family - an older man and woman. Soon after the bird left, the puppy next to me went away with a big family - a mom and dad with a little girl and a little boy. I couldn't help but wonder when MY family would come and who they would be.

As the day grew long, more and more of my friends left with their new families. Although they would be missed, I was very happy for them.

It was when the sun went down and it started to snow that I began to think that I would be spending Thanksgiving at Frank's.

Soon, I thought, *Frank will be sweeping the floors, shutting off the lights, and locking up the shop for the night.*

I was a bit sad, and even with some of my new friends still around me, I felt lonely. It helped me feel less sad and alone to think about who my new family might be.

I hope they come to find me soon!

Now earlier that very same day, the Nice Lady who lived on the other side of town was busy preparing for the Thanksgiving holiday. Most of the morning was spent baking pumpkin pies for her holiday dinner.

Finished with her baking, she wanted to take a break. She decided to meet her friend, the Farm Lady, for lunch. They agreed to meet at a quiet café so they could relax and talk about things that happened since they last met.

The Nice Lady had many things to talk about with her friend. She also had some additional shopping to do in preparation for tomorrow's Thanksgiving dinner.

Meeting the Farm Lady and finishing my shopping after our lunch together will be just perfect, thought the Nice Lady.

Soon after sitting down, the Farm Lady asked the Nice Lady how she was doing.

The Nice Lady said, "With Thanksgiving upon us, I have been thinking quite a bit about how blessed I am. I know I have many things in my life to be grateful for, like my family, friends, and my job, but I still feel like something is missing. With so much love and joy in my heart, I want to share my life with someone."

The Farm Lady said, "I totally understand, because even though I have my family and circle of friends, I find the love I share with the animals on the farm to be very special. You should think about getting a cat or a dog to care for and share your love. With so many homeless animals in need of rescue, perhaps you should go to a pet shelter. You just may find that special pet, waiting there for someone like you to give it a warm and loving home."

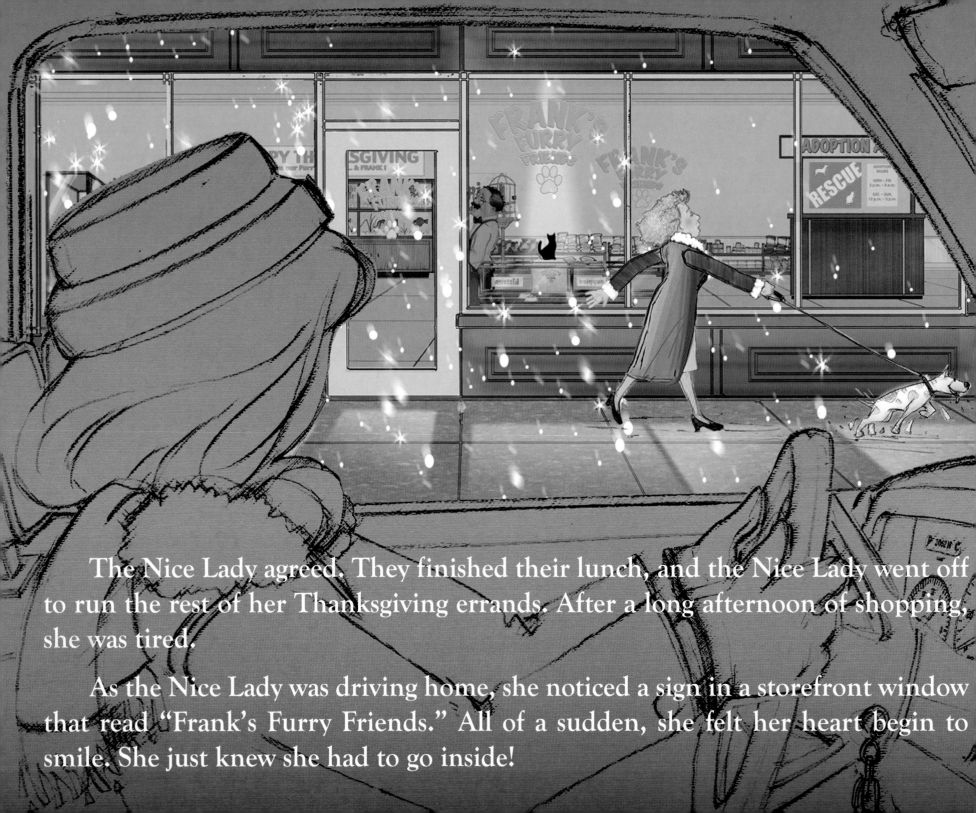

The Nice Lady agreed. They finished their lunch, and the Nice Lady went off to run the rest of her Thanksgiving errands. After a long afternoon of shopping, she was tired.

As the Nice Lady was driving home, she noticed a sign in a storefront window that read "Frank's Furry Friends." All of a sudden, she felt her heart begin to smile. She just knew she had to go inside!

With the shop about to close, the Nice Lady walked in to find Frank sweeping the floor.

He asked, "How can we help you?"

"I know it is late," said the Nice Lady, "but I was driving by and saw your sign and the little kitten in the window. May I meet him?"

"Sure," said Frank. "He could use a visitor right now. He is feeling a bit lonely since his sister and some of his furry friends left with their new families."

Just as I was curling up in my blanket, I saw this very Nice Lady walking towards me. Excitedly, I poked my head up high to smile at her, and at the same moment, I felt my heart begin to smile inside. When she picked me up and held me close, I felt so LOVED! I knew then I had found my family!

The Nice Lady held me close and told me she was bringing me home. We looked at each other and smiled.

With so many others having left that day with their new families, Frank was low on supplies. The only things left were a few cat toys and a cardboard box for me to sit in while riding to my new home. I didn't really mind, because I was leaving with this Nice Lady, who was now my family.

We got into her car, and she told me I would have to stay in the box so we'd be safe. I agreed, but I was so excited. I couldn't help wanting to look outside to see where we were going.

She had music on in the car, and she kept talking and telling me that it was "HER and ME!"

She said, "You're my Thanksgiving Cat, and I am so thankful I found you. I love your velvety, blue-gray fur. I always wanted a cat just like you!"

She told me she hadn't decided what name I should have, which was okay with me. I was just having fun riding in the car, listening to her sing, and watching the snow fall.

Once we arrived at my new home, I was so delighted I jumped out of my box and started to look around. The house felt very inviting and smelled very nice. I asked her, "What makes it smell so nice in here?"

She told me she had been baking pumpkin pies earlier that day for Thanksgiving. I followed the aroma into the kitchen, where I could better enjoy the smell of the pumpkin pies.

"I like this kitchen; it has lots of windows," I said.

"It gets very sunny and warm in here during the day," said the Nice Lady.

I thought, *I like this place already!*

In the next room I explored was this big cozy couch. I could tell it would be a perfect place for a nap. The Nice Lady picked me up and said, "I want to take you upstairs and show you where you'll be sleeping."

As we walked into this room, all I saw was a big, fluffy cloud. "Do you sleep on a cloud?" I asked her.

"No silly!" she said. "That's my bed, but it's like sleeping on a cloud."

We jumped up onto the bed; it was very soft. As she held me close, I felt very cozy, loved, and happy!

It was then I began to realize that all families are different. I had only one person in my family. Other animals at Frank's joined new families with two or more people. As I thought about how all families are different, the Nice Lady looked at me and said, "I am not sure why, but you just look like your name should be 'Nick'."

I told her I wasn't sure what kind of name I looked like, but if that's what she thought, I would be happy to take the name.

"It's perfect!" said the Nice Lady. "You are now officially Nick the Cat!" She picked me up and hugged me tight. She said she couldn't believe how fast the evening had rushed by. It was well after midnight.

"Happy Thanksgiving, Nick. It is now Thanksgiving Day!" she said.

She told me Thanksgiving wasn't just about the special dinner, pumpkin pie, or the treats. It was about being thankful for what you have... and thankful I was.

I was thankful my sister and friends at Frank's had found their new families. Most of all, I was thankful I had found someone to share life with and to be my family.

So, as the Wise Old Cat, I have learned that there are all kinds of families. Some families have a mom and a dad, and some have just a mom or just a dad. Other families have many sisters and brothers. Others have none.

Always remember: A family can be big or small, but most important, no matter what the size, it's your family.

So be very thankful for your
family and the love you share.

Did you enjoy this book? If so, be sure to look for my complete Nick the Cat Series offerings:

- 🤍 Series I - The Importance of Family - Publication Date: Fall 2009
    - Book I - How I Found My Family
    - Book II - How My Family Grew Overnight
    - Book III - How My Family Changed

Future Series Topics:

- 🤍 Series II - The Importance of Friendship - Publication Date: 2010 - 2011
- 🤍 Series III - The Importance of Our International Neighbors - Publication Date: 2011 - 2012
- 🤍 Series IV - The Importance of Being Green - Publication Date: 2012 - 2013
- 🤍 Series V - The Importance of Helping Others - Publication Date: 2013 - 2014

As with Series I, each of my future series will include three books full of value messages and life lessons for you young readers to grow by and cherish. Each book within each series will be published in six-month intervals which means no vacations for me anytime soon!

- Your friend, Nick

P.S.

🤍 Did you know that a portion of the proceeds from the sale of my books will be donated to Adopt a Pet in support of animal rescue in America? Being a rescued animal myself, I can tell you that every donation counts. If you would like to learn more about this very important organization and its mission, visit the AdoptAPet.com website. Also, all rescue shelters interested in fundraising activities through the sale of my books should visit my website, www.nickthecat.com for details.

🤍 Kids, for fun and interesting information about me and the Nice Lady – as well as information on release dates for future Nick the Wise Old Cat series books – you too, should visit my website, www.nickthecat.com from time to time. Also, when on my website, you can order my favorite illustrations that I have thoughtfully selected from my books to display in your room for you and your friends to enjoy. These illustrations are available either framed, framed and matted, or on stretched canvas. Each format illustration will be signed by my award–winning illustrator Dave Messing. He is a very "Nice Illustrator."

🤍 If you would like to have the Nice Lady read to you the three books on the Importance of Family, then you will love the CD that is also available on my website. Take it along with you when you and your family vacation by car or enjoy listening to it when you are at home. And while you're at it, Nick the Wise Old Cat plush toys can be ordered off my website if you have been unable to find them at your local bookstore.

And, of course, all merchandise available on my website is purrrrrfectly approved by me, as authenticated by my attached seal of approval.

purrrrrfectly
approved
by NICK

Whether you're reading to your child, grandchild, or the child within, you'll be enchanted by the endearing tales and amazing illustrations of this real-life nice lady and her real, four-legged family member. Endless thanks, Linda Sicks and Dave Messing, for sharing such a wonderful, much-needed affirmation of family — the key building block of society. What a great world this would be if more people heeded Nick's messages!

- Marybeth Dillon-Butler, author of the award-winning picture book
"Myrtle the Hurdler and her Pink and Purple, Polka-Dotted Girdle"

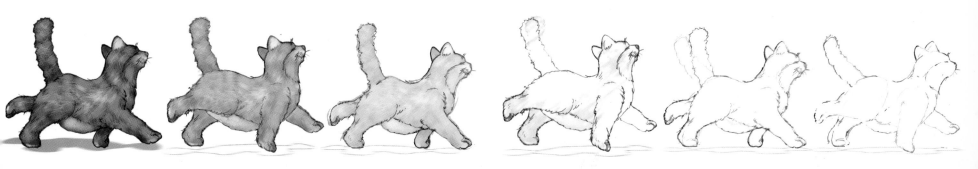